5 Minute Storytime

Children who are read to are inspired to read, so cuddle up for a **5 MINUTE STORYTIME** and expand your child's mind as you build a lifelong **LOVE** for reading and learning.

We cannot, however, guarantee your 5 minute break won't turn into 10, 15, or 30 minutes, as these **FUN** stories and engaging pictures will have you turning the pages **AGAIN** and **AGAIN**!

www.FlowerpotPress.com
DT-PAB-0909-0132
Made in China/Fabriqué en Chine

Chicken Little

A CAUTIONARY TALE

RETOLD BY
GEORGE BRIDGE

ILLUSTRATED BY
BEA MORITZ

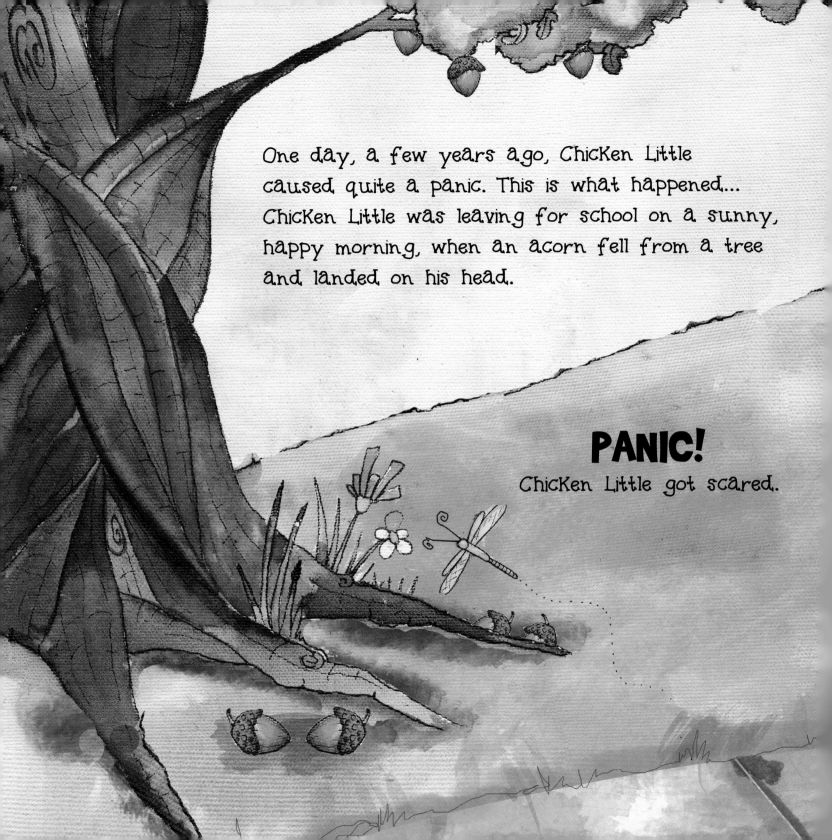

One day, a few years ago, Chicken Little caused quite a panic. This is what happened... Chicken Little was leaving for school on a sunny, happy morning, when an acorn fell from a tree and landed on his head.

PANIC!

Chicken Little got scared.

Henny Penny was walking to school when she heard the news.

PANIC!
She was really scared,
so she ran with her friend.

"The sky is falling!!!"
"The sky is falling!!!"
Chicken Little and Henny Penny
screamed as they ran.

"The sky is falling!!!"

"The sky is falling!!!"

Chicken Little, and Henny Penny,
and Turkey Lurkey screamed as they ran.

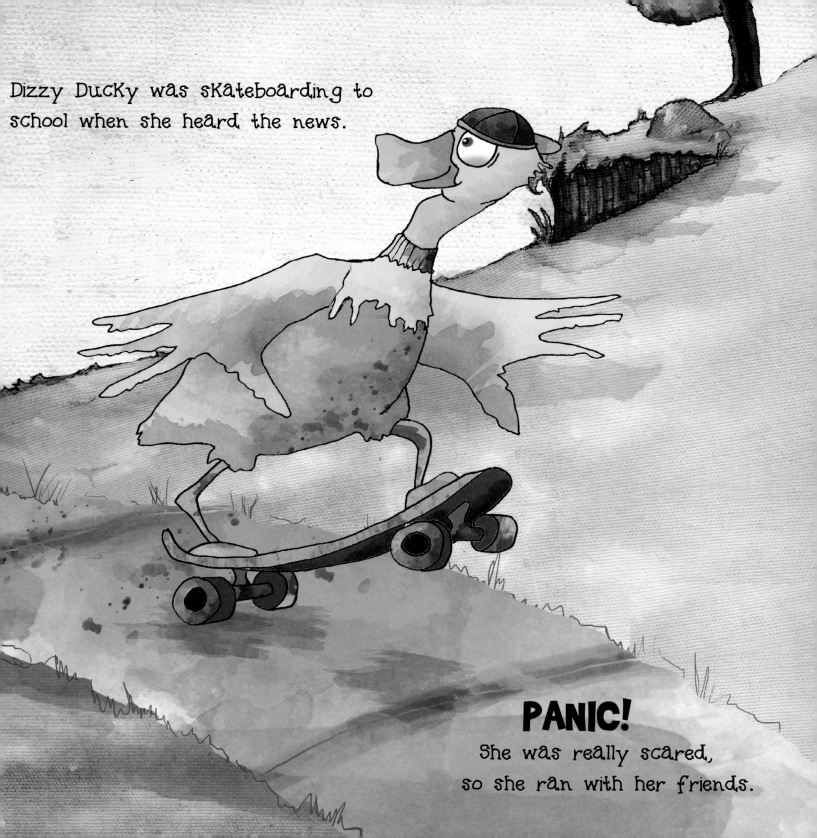

Dizzy Ducky was skateboarding to school when she heard the news.

PANIC!
She was really scared, so she ran with her friends.

Foxy Loxy was sitting outside his cave feeling hungry when he heard the news.

OPPORTUNITY!

He wasn't scared, but he was hungry.
"**RUN IN HERE!!! RUN IN HERE!!!**"
he screamed, and that is
just what the friends did.
"**NOW I'VE GOT YOU! FEED ME!**"
shouted Foxy Loxy
as he slammed the door.

Stuck inside the cave, the friends began to think. Then they began to talk. Then they began to figure out what had started the panic. Then they felt silly.

"**WE NEED to get out of here**,"
said, Chicken Little.
Now, instead of being scared, Chicken Little felt brave.
All of his friends followed Chicken Little
as he snuck out of the cave and into the sunshine.

Then they ran off to school.

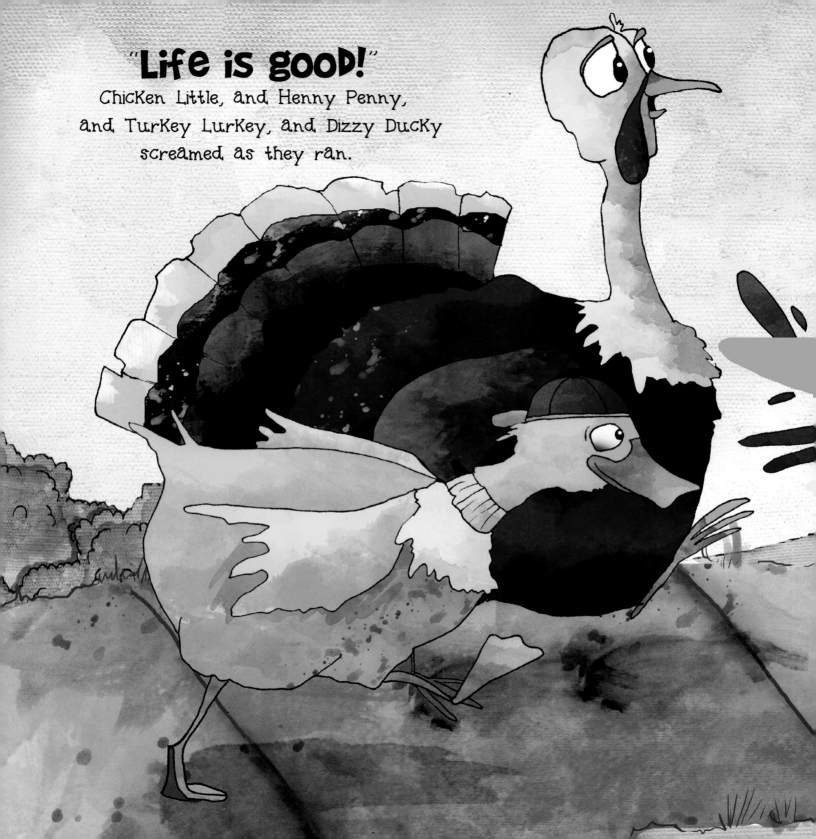

"**Life is gooD!**"
Chicken Little, and Henny Penny,
and Turkey Lurkey, and Dizzy Ducky
screamed as they ran.

And from that day forward, Chicken Little, and Henny Penny, and Turkey Lurkey, and Dizzy Ducky did not get scared so easily.

They did not panic. They knew that being brave and staying cool was way more fun!